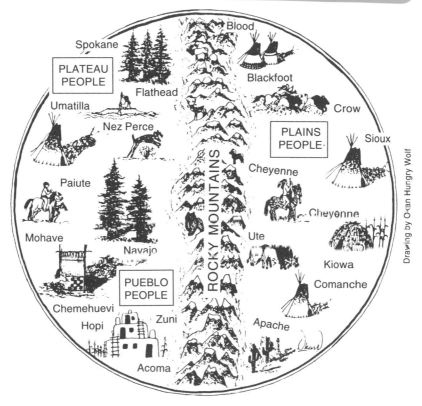

Spokane

PLATEAU PEOPLE

Umatilla

Flathead

Nez Perce

Blood

Blackfoot

Crow

PLAINS PEOPLE

Sioux

Cheyenne

Paiute

Cheyenne

Mohave

Ute

Navajo

Kiowa

PUEBLO PEOPLE

Comanche

Chemehuevi

Hopi

Zuni

Apache

Acoma

ROCKY MOUNTAINS

Drawing by Oksan Hungry Wolf

PREFACE

The tribes to which the children pictured in this book belong happen to be geographically located in a loose circle around Western North America. There is no real explanation for this — that's just the kind of photos that we've ended up with — yet, the circle is a most important spiritual and cultural symbol to life in traditional Native America, from which these scenes all come.

Circle of the Sun, Circle of the Moon, Circle of the Universe. Native philosophy says all life goes around in a circle, beginning with birth, changing through the seasons, always ending with death, from which will spring new life.

3

CONTENTS

CHILDREN
OF
THE
CIRCLE

By Adolf Hungry Wolf
and
Star Hungry Wolf

BOOK PUBLISHING COMPANY
SUMMERTOWN, TENNESSEE USA

GOOD MEDICINE BOOKS
SKOOKUMCHUCK, BC CANADA

ISBN 0-913990-89-2

Book Publishing Company
PO Box 99
Summertown, TN 38483 USA

Canadian ISBN 0-920698-37-9

Good Medicine Books
Box 844
Skookumchuck, BC V0B 2E0 Canada

Hungry Wolf, Adolf.
        Children of the circle : Indian kids in photographs / by Adolf and Star
Hungry Wolf.
            p.   cm.
        Includes index.
        ISBN 0-913990-89-2 : $9.95
        1. Indians of North America—West (U.S.)—Children—Pictorial works.
2. Indians of North America—West (U.S.)—Costume and adornment—Pictorial
works. 3. Indians of North America—West (U.S.)—Social life and customs—
Pictorial works. I. Hungry Wolf, Star. II. Title.
        E78.W5H948 1992
        306'.08997078—dc20   92-268
                                                                 CIP

Cover and text design by Eleanor Dale Evans

INTRODUCTION

As part of our family's cultural life, we have a large collection of old photographs showing Indian people, their camps, and scenes of many traditional activities. Among our favorites of these are ones that include native children, perhaps because four of them have grown up in our own household.

It would be wonderful if the photographers had left a lot of information with these old pictures. Instead, we are lucky when they have names, dates or tribal affiliations; many are just blank on the back. In this book, the title on each page will include whatever facts we have. After that, what we've written is based on our own research combined with thoughts and ideas inspired by our family's cultural life. These words are mainly presented for pleasure; the value of each photo speaks for itself.

Life for the Indian people of North America has changed a great deal since most of these pictures were taken. Instead of tipis, they now live in houses with tvs and running water. Instead of horses, they ride motorcycles and cars. Modern hunters get most of their food from supermarkets, while the girls use hair dryers and dream about favorite singing stars.

Yet, if you go to the tribes and locations mentioned in the titles, chances are you'll still find kids with pride in their traditional cultures. On special occasions, they might even be dressed as you see them in these pictures. We present this book most of all to encourage such kids in keeping alive their tribal cultures, while at the same time showing people of other cultures why Indian childhood is something to be very proud of.

Adolf & Star Hungry Wolf
Canadian Rockies - 1992

CROW GIRL
Crow Agency, Montana — c. 1920
Photo by Chapples, Billings, Montana

Dressed in her finest clothing and with earth paint on her face, we can assume that this girl has just gone through some kind of sacred ceremony. In the distant background appears to be a crowd gathered around an open shade of the kind often used during Crow Tobacco Society adoption rites, wherein new members are taken in by old ones who then treat them as if they were part of their own families. Perhaps this girl had just become a new member.

That the photographer was not very familiar with native culture is apparent by his note on the photo which says the girl is wearing an "Elk Tooth Dress." Such dresses have indeed been most highly valued among Crow women, but the decorations on this girl's dress are actually cowrie shells which are not nearly as valuable as elk teeth. The little cloth pouches attached to the shoulders of her dress contain medicine herbs that may have had special significance to the ceremony she just came from.

Notice that there are several horses standing nearby; probably these were being used as ceremonial payments. Proud parents who could afford to do so, gave away good horses in public to honor their children during ceremonial times such as this.

CROW GIRL
ELK TOOTH DRESS
© Chapples, Billings, Mont.

LITTLE CROW DANCER
Crow Agency, Montana — c. 1910

This young fellow must have been headed for a pow-wow dance out in the middle of camp when he got stopped to have his picture taken, probably at the back of his mom and dad's tipi. On his head is a porcupine-hair roach of the kind that men and boys often wear when they dance. Long ago, these were considered sacred headdresses, worn only by members of certain warrior societies. But since the end of the war-trail days they have become widely poplular among dancers of all tribes.

Calico shirts of the style he has on became common for Indian men and boys after cloth was made available at the trading posts; today they are still being worn. More rare is his necklace of glass tube beads, although similar styles are now made with modern materials. Notice how it ends with strings of smaller beads and little brass bells. We can just imagine the tinkling sounds he must have made when he hopped to the drum beats out on the dance ground. He would have been wearing a little short-cut breechcloth underneath his shirt.

MARK REAL BIRD — A LITTLE CROW DANCER
Crow Agency, Montana – c. 1915

Elderly warriors still performed traditional war dances at the time of this photo, but kids would not usually have taken part in them. Among the most popular Crow entertainments was the so-called Hot Dance, introduced a few years before this photo by members of the neighboring Hidatsa tribe. Although some sacred aspects of this dance would again have been done only by older people, it is possible that this boy was allowed to dress up and take part as sort of a "little friend." Such customs were common to most tribes, whose elders wanted to encourage their youths to keep alive the tribal heritage.

The buckskin jacket with beaded designs may well have been inherited, since it shows a lot of wear, although it might also have been his best suit for the past couple of years. Looks like he won't be wearing it much longer. The dance roach on his head, made from the long hair of a porcupine and the short hair of a deer's tail, took a lot of work and should last him a while, yet. A circular bustle of eagle feathers is tied at his back and straps of sleigh bells make noises when he moves his feet.

MAX BIGMAN AND HIS DANCING BOYS
Crow Indians from Lodge Grass, Montana — c. 1920
By Paul's Photos, Chicago

This noted leader of the Crow Indians is still remembered for bringing his boys to many places where they demonstrated native dancing while at the same time enjoying themselves immensely. Their clothing and dance styles were based on the ways of warriors from just before their father's generation, when the plains were still full of buffalo and enemies. Being coached by these old-timers, they formed a vital link in preserving tribal customs for today's native folk.

At first glance it seems that these boys are elaborately dressed, but if you look more closely you'll see that their outfits are made to be quickly outgrown. Only their cuffs are fully beaded; vests, moccasins and headbands are plain leather with a few beaded designs. The father's gear is more like that of a chief or leader, with lots of beadwork on his leather shirt and moccasins, plus an eagle tailfeather bonnet. This might have been at a country fair, where these three provided some extra entertainment.

VERONICA BAD BEAR AND DAUGHTER
Crow Tribe
Hardin, Montana – c. 1915

This picture is one of a series taken on the Crow reservation by some unidentified government employee. It's the only one that shows a kid, a little girl wearing a fancy cloth dress and bead earrings, plus a bunch of little braids in her hair. Having ridden in a blanket like this when I was little, here is what I imagine that kid to be thinking:

"Boy, I'm hot! Wonder why mom insists on making me ride up here in her blanket, instead of letting me run around in this white man's yard. Funny that the heat never seems to bother her — she wraps up in a blanket like this nearly every time we go outside, especially to town. Look at her, she's even got a scarf tied over her head as if it were freezing!"

CROW MOTHER AND DAUGHTER
Nellie Runs Between and her Mother, Kills Enemy
Crow Reservation – c. 1910

"This is where I come to watch my mother sew. That is how we learn; soon I will be able to help her with all that she does." That's the traditional way of growing up in a tribe, learning by watching and then doing. Nowadays, life is much more complicated; we don't learn so many things by watching our parents anymore.

This woman really loves her daughter, for she has made matching cowrie-shell dresses that they are both wearing. Cowrie shells are something like Indian jewelry, especially among the Plains people, who used to pay a lot to get them from ocean people by trade. Today we get them from craft shops instead, but they are still considered very special. My mom made a cowrie-shell dress for me a couple of years ago which I wear sometimes for dancing at pow-wows.

You might be interested to know something about their unusual names. At the time this picture was taken, the older people of many tribes still went by their Indian names, although the kids were usually given Christian names by the missionaries or at school. This girl's given name is Nellie; her father's Indian name would have been Runs Between, which his children then took on as their family name. Nellie most likely had her own Indian name, as well, probably given to her by some respected tribal elder. Often these names had to do with some dangerous adventure in the life of that elder — that's probably why Nellie's mom is called Kills Enemy. It was considered good luck for the name-giver to have survived his danger, so the naming was a form of blessing, or passing on that good luck.

"CARRYING PAPOOSE IN BLANKET"
Top-of-the-Forehead and her Grandson
Crow Agency, Montana – c. 1895

This old lady and her grandson probably didn't see many strangers around their prairie reservation home; from the looks on their faces they weren't used to having their picture taken either. Wonder what she's doing with the long end of her tack-decorated belt — perhaps her threat to use it is the cause of the kid's crying, or else he was scared of the photographer and his camera.

This was just a few years after the buffalo herds disappeared, so these people were dependent on rations given out by government employees at their agency. Each family recieved such basics as flour, beans, rice and fresh beef, enough to last them several days. Sometimes they also received material for clothing and blankets, such as the one she is wearing. Ration day would be the main time for a woman like this to make a trip in to the agency.

By the way, that's a real old style fur cap worn by the little kid, although it is made of sheepskin instead of the more common buffalo hide used in the past. It has a narrow browband of plain buckskin whose edge has decorative tabs cut into it. The old lady's cloth scarf would also have been made from soft bucksin in earlier times.

CROW BUDDIES
Crow Agency, Montana – c. 1908

The clothing worn by these boys represents several styles of ealy reservation dress which combines Crow traditions with store-bought items. Modernization goes outward; the guy in the middle looks most like an old-time Crow. He's the only one wearing earrings of round shells, a popular custom. His vest is fully beaded and there's also beadwork on his moccasins and hat. The guy to the left wears fully-beaded gloves, plus a plain cloth vest and an odd belt whose buckle looks like a watch. The boy on his other side wears a dark cloth vest with beaded flower designs, same as his moccasins. All four of the moccasin wearers also have the traditional Crow hairstyle for boys, three braids and a shortened forelock.

Maybe the fellow on the left went to a different school than the others, since he's made up as a European from head to foot, including a rather unusual pair of shoes. However, his appearance would not have prevented him from taking part in dances and other cultural events with his friends. Most likely he had some beaded clothing at home as well. This scene was taken in a Crow tipi camp during their summer vacation.

FOUR LITTLE SIOUX INDIAN GIRLS
By Paul's Photos, Chicago — c. 1920

Maybe these girls were in Chicago for a parade or some other special event, since they had along their nicest traditional clothes. The fully-beaded yokes of their dresses show that their parents were probably well-to-do and cared a lot for the girls. They also have fully-beaded moccasins and leggings, decorated with symbols and designs of their tribe.

Big studio, big city — how impressed and curious they must have been. Most likely this was their first visit to Chicago. Reservation towns back then would have consisted of a few dozen wooden buildings, including a general store or two, a ten-room hotel, a couple of restaurants, plus the government buildings. None of these would have been nearly as imposing as the hotel where they probably stayed while in the city.

Even today, country kids are usually fascinated by the sight of people and traffic from high up in a hotel room window. Imagine these four faces tightly squeezed together and staring at Roaring Twenties Chicago during the night time below with clattering streetcars, honking automobiles and masses of people. It would be quite a memory back out on the quiet, open prairie.

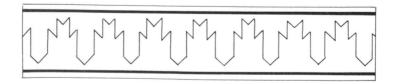

19

A SIOUX GIRL OF GREAT HONOR
Photo by Edward S. Curtis

Eagle plumes attached to her hair signify that this girl has gone through important tribal ceremonies that were also initiations to sacred ways for her to follow. She will wear the plumes on special occasions for the rest of her life, reminding her of the serious spiritual commitment she has made and letting other people know to treat her accordingly. Only a few girls had these experiences — the daughters of chiefs and successful families, or else poor girls of special promise that such persons sometimes chose.

One of the Sioux ceremonies symbolized by eagle plumes was called the "Hunkayapi" or "Waving the Horsetail," wherein the recipient was ritually adopted by the ceremony's sponsor, the resulting lifelong relationship being considered almost closer than actual family. The two agreed to share whatever they owned and to defend each other no matter what.

Since this girl wears more than one plume, it is likely that she received further initiations, such as the "Buffalo Sing," performed by noted medicine men and dreamers who were hired by wealthy parents when their daughters showed first signs of womanhood. The ceremony's main purpose was to encourage young women to be virtuous and upstanding, using buffalo symbolism to bestow blessings. To help celebrate their daughter's new status, parents gave away many posessions to the honored guests and others within the camp, to whom the girl was then formally considered a "Buffalo Woman."

SIOUX URCHINS

Miles City, Montana Territory — c. 1880
Photo by L.A. Huffman

The Battle of the Little Bighorn, with destruction of Custer and his troops, would have been a major event in the lives of these two Sioux kids, photographed just a few short years later by the same man who also took pictures of the leading chiefs in the battle, including Sitting Bull and Rain-in-the-Face. The girl might have told him:

"Our parents asked us to act honorable in your presence, because you have counseled with the chiefs. I even got to wear my big sister's dress and necklaces for this occasion.

"But my brother was not so willing to come along — look at him, he wouldn't even change into his nice clothing. He says he only came to protect me from you, 'cause you're a wasichu (paleface). He'd rather be out shooting gophers and playing war with his friends. But don't worry, he just acts big — he will not shoot you with his little arrows."

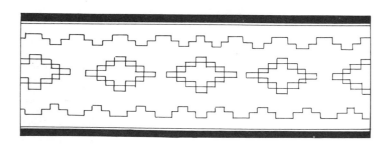

SIOUX BOY
c. 1900

"Aw, I suppose *you're* laughing at me too, back there behind your picture machine. Or else you're saying, 'Isn't he *cute!*' That's what my Grandma's friends say, when she brings me around in this dumb outfit to show me off.

"I don't care if this thing *is* fancy, with beads and stuff, other kids always laugh at me. See, right there's some of them looking because you're taking my picture. Boy, am *I* gonna get teased!

"Candy? What candy? Naw, I don't like them; especially not *your* kind. What kind is it? Let me see. You got more candy like this? The kind in the shiny wrappers? I *do* like them. I'll even tell you about my silly clothes for a few more of them.

"See, I'm the first-born in my family, which makes me pretty special. So my Mom and my Grandma worked together to make this outfit. See the colorful designs they beaded all over my vest and moccasins? Grandma made the pants from a young deerhide that she tanned especially soft for me, then she sewed the leaves on for deoration with flattened and dyed porcupine quills. That's the old time style from in the times before beads.

"*There*, now can you let me have the candies so I can go inside and change out of this?"

Two Sioux Boys
South Dakota — c. 1905

"I'm Sonny Swift Hawk, and I'm a Rosebud Sioux. My dad is Eldon Swift Hawk, but he hardly cares for that name, except at ration time, when the government people read from the food list. He doesn't speak English, but he knows when they call his name. Among our people he is called Striped Face, not Eldon Swift Hawk, but we only call him that in our language. Swift Hawk, in our language, was the name of *his* father. The government people added Eldon and said it was his name.

"Striped Face means Badger, so actually my father's name in English should be Badger. He has mystery powers from Badgers, that's how he got the name. I can't explain it to you, but he speaks to them in his dreams. You see, we live way out here on the Plains, and there are Badgers all around us. They have given my father Power which helps him to cure people. He has made my sicknesses go away since I can remember.

"My parents call me by the name Only Boy, although I have recently been given a warrior's name as well, for good luck. But I'm not allowed to say this one out, because it's for later in my life...

"This fully-beaded suit was made by my Grandma, who is called Meadowlark. She cried when I first came back home from school with my hair cut. Even now, a year later, she still gets upset about it, especially when we're alone and I sit on her lap. She always used to comb my hair when it was long, and then she would braid it real nicely.

"I'm Grandma's favorite in the family. That's why she made me this fancy beaded suit. I don't mind wearing it for her, because she worked long and hard at it. You see how tiny these beads are? There are nearly as many as the grass out here on our pasture, and she sewed them all on by hand. That's pretty good, considering her old eyes. She said to my folks: 'The white men can cut his hair and make him wear their kind of clothes at school, but they cannot stop me from putting beads on my grandson so that he will not forget that he's still an Indian!'

"This here's my friend, Yellow Antelope, though at school we call him Charley. I forgot what his last name is, I just remember Charley. He's got a Grandma too. She's my Grandma's best friend. Right now they're back in the cabin, visiting together.

"This thing in my hand, that's *my* Grandma's gun, though his Grandma carries one, too. There's been a couple of old ladies robbed and even killed, mostly when they went into town with money. So a lot of them now carry little guns like this — just as if they were in the warrior societies, like our dads.

"We're gonna use it for hunting, instead! Us two are gonna be hunters! Our Grandmas said we could borrow it and shoot them a couple of big prairie dogs. They said they'd cook them and we'd all have an old-time feast. Better than bacon from those pigs at the ration house. We know right where to go for them, too. Just stick around here a while till we get back, you'll see!"

LOVELY KATIE
Rosebud Sioux, South Dakota — 1898
Photo by John A. Anderson, Nebraska State Historical Society
Azusa Postcard

This seems like a Rembrandt among the photos of native Indian childhood. Such a nice looking girl, so perfectly dressed in her beaded buckskin outfit, standing on her people's version of a "red carpet" — a buffalo robe overlayed with an almost-fully beaded saddle blanket. Even the painted statue on the backdrop seems awed by the little girl's presence; the doll looks delighted.

This is Katie Roubideaux at age 8, the daughter of a Sioux mother and Louis Roubideaux, a noted mixed blood who served as official interpreter on the Rosebud Reservation and was at one time captain of the Indian Police. Later, upon marriage, she became Katie Roubideaux Blue Thunder, a highly respected woman who lived into great old age.

"BOYS' DORMITORY"
Sioux Tribe, Fort Totten, North Dakota - c. 1900

This is the first of a set of three photos taken at the same time and location showing different aspects of boarding school life at the turn of the last century. Thousands of Indian boys and girls lived through scenes like this, learning strange things and a different way of life, their hearts often in pain from loneliness and a strong yearning to be back in their tribal homes with their own families.

The fathers and grandfathers of these Sioux boys still wore their hair mostly in braids, spending much of their time trying to keep alive tribal traditions, while government laws forced them to give up their children during the vital learning years. These boys are from an era when heroes would have been those same fathers and grandfathers, many of whom had fought for their people against numerous enemies.

Putting aside thoughts of the obvious tragedy this new system brought to their tribal heritage, most of these students left school better prepared for dealing with the dominating world that surrounded them. Many successful boarding school students returned to their tribal culture in time, their more modern outlook helping to bring about changes that have resulted in people like the Sioux still maintaining their heritage near the year 2000.

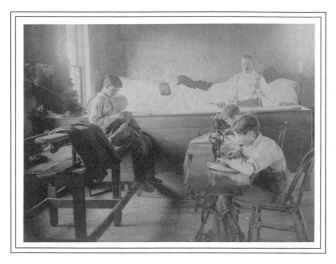

"TAILOR SHOP"
Sioux Tribe, Fort Totten, North Dakota - c. 1900

Their forefathers might have considered this women's work, but while in boarding school every boy was expected to mend his own clothing and sew perfect seams. The husky teacher in back was probably a firm disciplinarian, since school punishments were often in the form of strappings. Many native parents were quite upset to learn that their children were punished in this way. For one thing, native customs frowned upon anyone hitting children. More importantly, hitting someone else in tribal life was very serious and generally led to fighting or war.

At home, learning tribal ways would be encouraged by thoughts of success, whereas at school it would be to avoid the punishment that usually followed failure.

"AT SUPPER"
Sioux Tribe, Fort Totten, North Dakota — c. 1900

At the end of the buffalo era, just a few years before this picture was taken, the parents and grandparents of these kids would have been grateful for the good meal that is probably about to be served. In those times the people had much difficulty adapting from their constant hunting and eating of wild animals to being totally dependent upon government rations which might be unclean and often consisted of raw foods whose ways of preparation were unknown or considered strange tasting.

Social discipline at this school was more relaxed than at many others, where boys and girls were not allowed to sit at the same tables or even talk to each other. Mind you, some tribal custom traditions were equally strict; mothers and grandmothers keeping a stern eye upon the girls to make sure no boys fooled around with them. This usually started at the end of childhood, involving unmarried men and women, especially brothers and sisters.

"AT PLAY"

"Recess, No. 2 Day School, Standing Rock Reservation"
Sioux Tribe, North Dakota — c. 1900

Taken at about the same time as the previous three photos, this shows a group of Sioux girls from a neighboring reservation. Instead of having to live at boarding school, these girls were fortunate to attend classes in the daytimne and be home with family at night. Sometimes parents moved into cabins surrounding these day schools, which was more convenient all around.

Perhaps the photographer has allowed these girls to play with his buggy, while his blonde-haired son sits proudly as the center of attention. For these Indian children it would be an unusual experience to have such a light-skinned playmate. He would have been a topic of conversation for days afterward.

"SCHOOL POLICEMAN"
"No. 2 Day School, Standing Rock Reservation"
Sioux Tribe, South Dakota — c. 1900

This man had to be very brave, to face down his fellow tribesmen, the most conservative of whom often tried to keep their children at home and out of the white man's schools. Notice that he carries a gun, presumably for self-defense. Ironically, just in recent years some school policemen are again being armed, though this time for much different reasons, to protect themselves and others from dangerous youths.

As tribes were settled on their reservations in the second half of the 1800's, they were forced to accept goverment laws that severely restricted their lives and included the taking away of school-age children. Besides the three R's, Indian education usually covered such topics as gardening and livestock care, cooking and household work, plus shop classes like carpentry and sewing.

Students learned to be self-sufficient, gaining valuable experiences that were replaced more and more by straight desk learning as the decades went by. Although the drop-out rate is still unusually high for native students, more and more are earning university degrees, their school experiences being quite far removed from those known to the kids that this man dealt with.

"UNCIVILIZED"
Sioux — c. 1910

It's obvious that the photographer and the parents saw two different things in this little boy — for one of them he was pride and joy, while the other looked upon him only as a quaint and curious photo subject. With such a sarcastic title, perhaps it's just as well that the photographer did not leave us his name or other details.

Looking carefully at this scene, the boy's parents appear to be watching from the background, dressed in modern fashion and taking a break from their agricultural pursuits.

Perhaps he was the family favorite to have such a fancy traditional outfit, which he would not have been wearing all the time. Besides the beadwork on his hatband, vest, leggings and moccasins, there is a quill-decorated robe at his feet of the style that often signified a special child. In addition, the pinto horse was probably his, perhaps a gift from an indulging grandfather or some other admirer.

A VISIT TO THE STUDIO
Cheyenne, Montana — c. 1880

Do you suppose these two Cheyenne girls understood why the photographer went to all the trouble to put a painted scene in his studio, when he could have come out to their reservation and photographed them with the real thing?

The girl on the couch could have been thinking, "Hmm, handsome fellow, this photographer, but strange ways." Maybe he had hair on his face, too, something neither of them would be accustomed to.

The elk teeth on their dresses indicate they were from well-off families. Probably they were from the hunts of a father, brother or other caring hunters. How do you suppose they felt about them compared to someone like the photographer?

CHEYENNE BOY
c. 1878

This is one of the earliest portraits taken of an Indian boy on the Great Plains, somewhere around the time of the big battle with Custer's troops, in which the boy's tribe came out victorious. The battle would have been a major topic for him and his playmates throughout their growing up years.

Lacking bicycles and other toys of modern childhood, young native kids usually played with smaller versions of adult tools, such as this boy's bow and arrows. Note that there is a leather wrist guard on his left arm, which indicates that he was not just holding the weapon for his photograph. The two arrows have sharp metal points which would have brought down most prey, including human enemies. It is hard for us today to imagine life back then, with potential dangers at every bend in the trail, even in the brush behind his family's tipi.

Another tremendous difference in life back then were the extreme weather changes — hunters often being caught out in hard rainstorms or raging winter blizzards dressed only in their leather clothing, without such comforts as woolen socks or long underwear. However, native kids grew up to be hearty, dressed in very little for much of the time, as you can see here from this boy's breechcloth. The bone and bead breastplate was more a symbol of pride and male adornment than anything practical. He also wears several silver hoops for earrings.

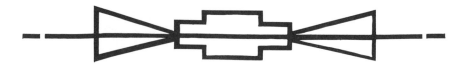

THREE GENERATIONS OF CHEYENNE WOMEN
Stone Calf's Wife, Daughter and Granddaughter
Lame Deer, Montana — c. 1895
Photo by George Bird Grinnell.

Stone Calf was a noted leader of the Northern Cheyenne who took part in many battles as well as peace councils. We might imagine that this scene by his tipi shows the three women closest to him in life, perhaps watching as he rides off to another adventure.

These three must have spent a lot of time together inside their tipi home, beading, sewing and cooking on an open fire — much of the time visiting with each other and those who might stop by. Grown women usually went around wearing blankets, like these two, even while they were working. They might drop the top half over belts around their waists for convenience. They kept blankets at hand in place of jackets or sweaters.

Because of the formal posing commonly used by photographers in those days, we do not often see the love shown in this photo, yet Indian children were commonly treated with great affection by their elders.

41

CHEYENNE MOTHERS
DIGGING FOR ROOTS
Lame Deer Agency, Montana – c. 1890
Photos by George Bird Grinnell

"Going for the Groceries" could be another title for these scenes. This is how kids in the old days rode with their Moms and Grandmas when they went out from camp to dig roots and other plants. Perhaps they were as excited riding along behind horses as little kids today are when going for a drive in the family car. "Oh, what fun!" sings one of the children happily.

The woman in the foreground, wearing a fancy shawl, is leaning forward with her sturdy stick to pry loose what? Maybe a wild turnip or carrot, both of which were common traditional foods. She'll bake these over coals in the ground, like a primitive oven. They were baked day and night until they got soft and juicy. They made a welcome addition to the basic meals of plain wild meat.

Maybe the woman is looking for medicine roots instead, which she'll boil into teas, or apply over wounds and sores to make them get better. Going on a root digging and plant gathering trip like this was like getting groceries and visiting the drug store at the same time.

The kids must have liked their travois seats, which were never quite completely still. A travois was the old time trailer, made from wooden poles tied at the tips and slung across the horse's shoulders. Crosspieces were tied on behind and covered with padding to provide a seat, or else a platform on which to tie the household belongings whenever camp was moved. Maybe when these women sit down for a break, the kids will get off and search around the ground for interesting rocks or insects.

43

TANGLE HAIR AND HIS GRANDDAUGHTER
Northern Cheyenne Reservation, Montana Territory – c. 1895

What was this girl thinking, while she sat by her famous grandfather and watched him smoke a pipe? No doubt he mentioned her in the prayers he would have said while blowing puffs of smoke in the various directions of the universe — pipe smoking was always a ceremonial act for people like him, especially when they used their long-stemmed, decorated pipes kept in special bags like his with the big panel of beadwork.

Perhaps Tangle Hair's grandaughter was old enough to understand that he would have smoked this pipe — or one like it — with various enemies over the course of his life, each time to celebrate the making of peace and friendship. It was this important purpose of smoking that led to the common name "peace pipe."

But not all of Tangle Hair's experiences were peaceful and the girl surely knew about. As leader of the Cheyenne "Dog Soldiers" — a brave and feared warrior society — he battled with enemies from such tribes as the Crow and Pawnee. But his grteatest tests came while helping to protect Cheyenne women and children from the numerous attacks by U.S. army troops who were determined to force these people to stop roaming their traditional hunting country and settle down, instead, on plots of land designated as reservations by the government. He would have had many sad stories to tell of his poeple's sufferings and defeats against cruel and overwhelming odds. He lived to tell those stories until 1911, when he died of quite an old age.

45

Two Cheyenne Girls
Lame Deer, Montana – c.1910

These girls are not only dressed up in their fancy clothing, they also have their faces painted, which means it was a very special day for both of them. Back in those times such facial paintings were given during the course of sacred ceremonies, such as a medicine bundle opening or a Sun Dance. It was the sign of honored blessings, native paint from the Earth, applied by a priest or priestess of the people. A sign of faith in the powers of earth and nature.

Dentalium shells decorate the wool dress of the girl on the left. These are like Indian pearls, usually obtained by trade from other tribes nearer the west coast, where the shells were eagerly sought. The women of many tribes decorated their dresses with them; for a little girl they would have been a very special treat.

The other girl wears a breastplate of hairpipes made in a style commonly worn. Although made of bone and thought to be traditional native work, these hairpipes werre actually produced by European craftsmen and brought to Indians by traders. Both girls wear belts decorated with conches which were probably made by native artists, who learned this craft from the traders from whom they obtained the metal.

HOME ON THE RANGE
Southern Cheyenne, Oklahoma — c. 1885

This photo gives some feeling of the vastness on the Southern Plains of Oklahoma, where part of the great Cheyenne tribe was forced by government troops to settle. They hadn't been there very long when this photo was taken, as can be seen from the native clothing styles, especially the leggings and breechcloth worn by the man in the background carrying a very primitive ladder. These four girls would have had little idea of the greater world that lay beyond their prairie country, which must have seemed world enough to them.

CHANGING TIMES
Southern Cheyenne, Oklahoma — c. 1890
George Bird Grinnell Photo

These girls were among the first generations of Cheyennes to grow up on reservations, where life was really different from before. Notice that they're still going around with shawls instead of jackets or coats. Even if they were attending the agency school already, they probably dressed like this when they were at home with their family. The two outside girls are wearing simple cloth dresses, while the middle girl wears a beaded and decorated one of buckskin without a shawl.

CAUGHT BY THE FLASH

Southern Cheyenne, Oklahoma — c. 1890
Photo by George Bird Grinnell

"Say Cheese," must not have meant much to these three kids, from their cheese-less expressions. Imagine being their age and having hardly ever smiled for a camera — this could have been their very first photo. Around the time they were born, their people still tried to follow their original tribal life on the open plains, but they were frequently hunted by army troops because of this yearning for freedom. No doubt, these kids lost family members during the years of constant skirmishes, which affected everybody.

CHEYENNE BROTHER AND SISTER
Oklahoma Territory — c. 1890
Photo by George Bird Grinnell

These children lived in a time before boys had to cut their hair for school and when clothing like this was still part of their regular life. Most men and boys also still wore earrings as a traditional custom, such as the silver dangles in this case, but outside influence later made them ashamed of it.

From the handsome appearance of their clothing it is apparent that these two belonged to a successful family, although the Cheyennes have always been noted for their personal pride. The dentalium shells were among native life's most delicate trade goods and valuables, coming from tribes who lived along the ocean. The boy's armbands are from a special metal called German silver, the fine engraving of which is a noted art in the Southern Plains where they were living. The beads on his head are for decorating his hair.

UTE MOTHER AND SON
Durango, Colorado — 1910

The place where this picture was taken is today a world-famous tourist town, but not too long before it was in the heart of these people's domain. Several bands of Utes roamed through the Rocky Mountain country of Colorado, Utah and New Mexico, proud of their tipi-dwelling and buffalo-hunting ways. This woman may have known the last of those free days, but her boy probably had to take off his fancy gear after this picture and get back to reservation school life.

Otters are highly-regarded animals in native culture, so this boy's otter neckpiece was no doubt a prized item in his family. Based on its size, it probably looked much better on his dad, who might have been watching this scene with delight from nearby.

KIOWA BOY AND GIRL
Indian Territory — c. 1890

This is one of those intriguing old-time pictures that says so much and yet has absolutely no information written on the back. We know they are Kiowa from their particular style of dress — especially the boy's well fringed buckskin suit with its bead-designed legging tabs flapping to the front. Also his bead-and-otterfur braid wraps, a variation of which was used by the boys and men of numerous tribes. The girl wears a light cotton print shawl, wrapped as an apron, over her ribbon-edged cloth dress.

"Little husband and wife" is the imaginary title we give this picture, since it makes us think of stories in which children were sometimes promised to each other for marriage at a very early age, occasionally even before they were born. If ths couple was one of them, they were not necessarily married yet. Their fathers might have been two lifelong best friends who made the marriage promise between themselves, even if the kids weren't of the same age. Such a promise created a special bond between the families. Perhaps on this day their parents got the kids posed, figuring someday this picture would be special.

KIOWA GIRL NAMED FLATFOOT
Anadarko, Oklahoma, Indian Territory — c. 1890

Flatfoot actually seems to have flat feet, since her smoked-hide moccasins are pretty wide, but she looks pretty and proud anyway. The long fringes on her white buckskin dress are typical for her people.

That the Kiowa were then learning to walk two roads — their own traditional one and the newly-arrived "white man's" — is symbolized by two sacred articles that she wears side by side on her chest. One is a small cloth pouch probably containing some kind of herbal medicine — sacred to life in nature — the other is a cross representing the new religions practiced inside of churches.

We wonder how the Kiowa first reacted to the story of Adam and Eve, since their own origin legend says that Kiowa ancestors came to this Earth through a hollow log. Girls like Flatfoot would have called themselves "Kwuda," which means "Coming Out" in their own language and refers to that time of origin.

The Kiowa have always been a small tribe, which is explained in the same legend. Among the first people coming out from the hollow log was a pregnant woman who got stuck, thereby keeping the rest of the tribe back. Still, the Kiowa were widely respected and even feared across the Plains.

KIOWA BOY NAMED GEORGE MILES
Anadarko, Oklahoma Territory — c.1890

Old traditions recall the Kiowa being mountain people living along the Northern Rockies of Montana, before they migrated down to the hot Southern Plains, learning many customs and ceremonials from other tribes along the way.

When they reached the southernmost parts of their range along the Mexican border, some curious Kiowas decided to go find out how much further it was from there to "the home of the Sun." They were obviously much closer than before, since the days were longer and often hotter.

Eventually this brave group of fellows reached forests more thick and wet than any they'd imagined. One night they heard strange sounds from above, like the chatterings of little people. By the light of dawn they saw them climbing among the trees. But strangest of all was that they had long tails! That was too much for the Kiowa warriors who turned back to their open land of plains and gladly left the dense, wet jungles behind.

The heroes of Kiowa boys were members of a warrior society called the "Real Dogs." There could be only ten living members at a time, and they were the tribe's bravest. Treated with great respect by everyone, they wore fancy long sashes as badges of honor. When the tribe was attacked, these men pinned their sashes to the ground with sacred arrows and vowed to stand in defense until the end.

Kiowa clothing includes a lot of sashes, fringes and other hanging things. This boy is wearing a buckskin suit with long twisted fringe down the front, along with otterskin braid wraps that hang nearly to his ankles. He was surely the son of proud parents.

CHIEF BIG TREE'S DAUGHTERS
Kiowa — c. 1880

These two sisters look so much different from each other because they probably had different mothers.

Big Tree was a noted Kiowa chief whose position would have allowed him several wives. Also befitting the family of a chief, both girls are well-dressed in traditional style, with the one on the right having elk teeth (the Indian "diamonds") above her belt of conches.

The girls would have known their father as Adoeette, which means Big Tree in Kiowa. He was born about 1845 and became a noted warrior and chief during the final battles his tribe fought with enemies. From his reservation lands in Oklahoma he led Kiowa war parties down into Texas to raid wagon trains and settlers that were invading their territory. He was imprisoned at Ft. Sill, Oklahoma, where two fellow chiefs died. Later he adapted to reservation life, learned about Christianity, and took care of his family until his death in the early 1900's.

CHIEF BIG TREE'S DAUGHTERS.

61

"ANNA & DENISE —
KIOWA COUSINS"
Indian Territory, Oklahoma — c. 1890

It's easy to tell that one of these girls is more shy than the other. In this era they may not have even spoken English, nor would they have seen many outsiders like this photographer. The braver girl seems quite curious; she was probably looking up into the photographer's face, as he towered above the camera and squeezed the shutter for this picture. Here's what we'd imagine them to be saying:

"Oh look Anna, this white man is going to put us on one of those papers, like the one we have at home of mother and father. Soon we'll be able to see ourselves without using a looking glass!"

"That's fine for you Denise, but I'm *still* scared of bushy faces! It's not so bad when he's underneath that black cloth, but I don't like it when he comes back out and makes faces at us; I want to just run away."

"Oh Anna, don't be silly. When did you ever hear of a bushy face hurting a kid? They only look that way because...because they're different. What if father could grow hair like that and become a bushy face, would you still be scared? Maybe this man's kids would be scared of father's long hair, or laugh at the way we wear our shawls around our waists."

Both girls are wearing open-sleeved dresses made of velvet, perhaps dark blue, red or green, which were the popular colors. Their woven sashes were probably obtained from another tribe by trade, as they were mostly made further north from the Kiowa Southern Plains country.

"KIOWA - COMANCHE FAMILY"
"MAGGIE, HENRY AND DICK WHITE CALF"
"4th of July Pow-Wow Camp"
Oklahoma — c. 1910

There were no dates or calendars in the old time Indian way of life, although the passing moons were carefully observed, along with the seasons. After the start of reservation life, many U.S. tribes made a main event each year out of the country's national holiday, July 4th.

This family is camped with relatives and friends in a traditional circle of tipis and tents, away from town and their ordinary cabins, with tribal dress being worn instead of the everyday government-issued clothing. The time in camp is spent visiting, singing songs, performing various dances and in general keeping alive the spirit of their tribe.

The little girl is still too young for school, so she probably thinks this is what life is all about. Her beaded moccasins and vest (perhaps outgrown by an older brother) will become fond memories once she starts studying schoolbooks.Yet, what she's experiencing here with her parents will remain in her heart — as it did for so many other native people, allowing them to return to their culture in later life if they wished to.

"COMANCHE BOY"
Wellington, Kansas – c. 1895
Photo by E.B. Snell, Elite Gallery

This was sure somebody's special child, by the neat way he is dressed. Perhaps his dad was an important person in the tribe, his mom a proud and pretty lady.

The photo was taken in a studio, away from their reservation. The light calico shirt must have been new; it is so long that it also serves as an apron down over his fancy, wide-flapped woolen leggings. Around his neck is a choker of dentalium shells and across his store-bought vest he has a bandolier of hairpipes and brass beads plus a fine metal chain that might have a bag at the end. His long hair is wrapped with otter fur and he also has on a fancy pair of silver earrings.

GIRL OF THE SOUTHERN PLAINS
c. 1880

From the age of this photo we can assume the girl posed here is in her everyday dress, or at least her *good* everyday dress. Even the black-striped blanket could have been part of her regular wear, since it was still the custom for most native people then to wear blankets instead of jackets. It and the beads she wears would have come from a trading post, but all her other clothing is homemade.

The dress in the picture is basically a fringed gown with shoulder straps of a style thought to have been worn all over the Plains in times before the arrival of horses and white men. In warm weather it was worn by itself; a shoulder cape such as seen here was put on whenever it was cool enough. Before beads, such capes would have been decorated with porcupine quillwork, or left plain for everday cooking and tanning work.

"JICARILLA APACHE HALF-BREED"
"JESUS WITH HIS DAUGHTER"
Dulce, New Mexico — 1907

Could this have been one of the first baby strollers used on an Indian reservation? Other pictures of Apaches from around this time show kids still being carried in cradleboards. But then, this is a half-breed's child — a proud looking father with sort of a European face in addition to his long, traditional braids. Maybe even *he* rode in a stroller — bought by his white dad — back when he was small.

This man is of a generation that might have tasted wild buffalo meat, too, but his little girl probably grew up eating mostly beef, or deer meat that her dad might have hunted. Yet, she would probably still spend a lot of time during nice weather around a tipi, although her folks appear to have a log house. Back then, most Apache families still used tipis for summer camping or for travelling to other places. Some Canadian tribes continued this custom until just a few years ago. Even now, most former tipi-dwellers, including the Apaches, still camp in them sometimes.

The Jicarilla are one of the better known groups of Apaches. Their name means "little basket" because they were so good at basket making. They used to hunt buffalo out on the Southern Plains and camp along the Rio Grande River. They also lived from cactus gathering in the hot desert sands. They were related to another famous desert tribe, the Navajo, both of them originally coming down from the cold far north, where their relatives to this day are the numerous Dene people.

REUBEN SPRINGER'S WIFE AND CHILDREN
Jicarilla Apache — 1909

"I'm shy! I want my picture taken, but I'm shy to look at you. Why? 'Cause you've got such a hairy face! How do you make all that hair grow on your face? Does your wife have that, too? And your babies, do they have bushy faces?

"Yeah, Reuben is my dad. Where is he? He's right over there, behind you. He's making faces at me, and he's making bigger faces at Mama. He putting his lips out like he's gonna kiss Mama; I think she's gonna laugh in just a minute.

"What was I doing before you came here? I was helping my mom work. We're tanning this hide. It's a cow hide we got down at the agency. Mom says this is how they used to tan buffalo hides when *she* was a little girl. I never saw a buffalo, have you? My dad says they have faces like our agent, big beards like yours. Are you a buffalo man?

"No, it doesn't rain through the roof of our house. This tipi isn't our house. That's our log house over there, behind my dad. This tipi is just for us to play in; I mean, *work* in. My mom and I sit in there and rest, when we've worked on this hide long enough. See, we have it stretched out, and we're scraping all the meat and fat off its inside. Then we'll turn it over and scrape off the hair, unless my mom decides to make a rug out of it, then she'll leave the hair on. Would you like to have somebody make a rug out of *you?*"

HAPPY CHILDHOOD DAYS
Pueblo de Taos, New Mexico — c. 1910
By Paul's Photos, Chicago, Illinois

One white man, seen through another white man's eyes, while the first white man is busy filming "a couple of little Indians." These gentlemen probably travelled out to the pueblo in a wagon or buggy, wanting to record what they figured may not be seen again.

When I was little I remember visiting distant relatives at Taos pueblo, where life still seemed about the same as this. Some women come to mind, whom I watched as they baked native bread in big round adobe ovens. On the tops of ancient houses including this one, there were many dozens of color-fully dressed people one day, looking down into the old village plaza, where my brothers and I — along with our parents — mingled among the many excited participants at a Feast Day Festival.

There was a strong-willed old woman who was the grandmother in the household of our relatives. She left a particular impression on me. At the age of almost 100, she was still determined to live in the simple family pueblo house of her ancestors, even though strict village laws allowed no electricity, running water or indoor plumbing, and she had just lost both her legs to an old age ailment.

Although she had a World War II veteran son living in a very modern and comfortable home not far away, she chose to spend her final season within the old village walls, among the ceremonials of her ancient culture.

74

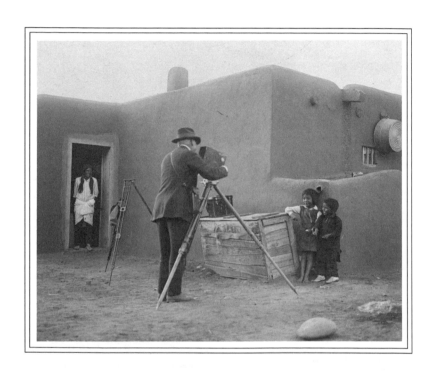

"PUEBLO INDIAN"
New Mexico — 1895

Here's a typical scene at one of the New Mexico pueblos showing a mother taking a break from her busy day to nurse one of the three little boys being looked after by their older sister. In traditional native life, little kids were mostly cared for by their older siblings — even cousins or young aunts — while the parents were occupied with the families' everyday needs. Adult supervision and instruction was often given by grandparents or other family elders who had retired from more active life.

The play of Indian children usually imitated the work of adults, so it was not difficult for them to adjust from one stage to the other. For instance, this girl might have played with dolls in her free time and considered her duties here as a step closer to adulthood. Note that her dress and appearance is already similar to her mother's. At ceremonial times she would have been allowed to dress up and dance with her mother, as well.

An Indian Family - New Mexico. 1895

TURKEY DANCERS AND THEIR TEACHER
Santa Clara Pueblo, New Mexico
c. 1920

The Pueblo people have many ceremonial dances that honor different things in nature. These two boys are learning to imitate wild turkeys, which provided hunters with a good supply of meat and feathers for their families. Some of these feathers are attached to the wings on these boys, while from their belts hang numerous turkey beards. Kilts, body paintings and interesting headgear complete their outfits.

The old man in the background holds a stick in his right hand which he's beating on the slender drum in his left. My brother Okan knew an elderly man from this same pueblo who adopted him as a grandson and showed him a ritual with corn, another important gift from nature for which his people performed ceremonial dances.

Notice this man's traditional clothing, which is different from that of pueblos further south. Santa Clara men used to go buffalo hunting with friendly Plains tribes, learning to dress somewhat like them in the process.

HAPPY DAY AT ZUNI PUEBLO
New Mexico — 1907

This scene could be the setting of a fairy tale — a place of mystery and excitement. Indeed, Zuni Pueblo has existed for many centuries during which all sorts of dramatic events took place. Among them are daily ceremonial meetings in underground chambers called kivas, where only the initiated may enter. These same people — men, women and children — take turns performing ceremonial dances in colorful sacred costumes, with spectators watching from roof tops like those seen here. All the places would be packed with people looking down into the village plaza.

"Hey you guys, another photographer," these kids are probably saying in their own language, knowing that candy treats often follow smiling for pictures. Nowadays, many pueblos have standard fees for outsiders wanting to bring cameras, though some forbid this during ceremonial events, while others no longer allow picture taking at all.

HOPI GRANDFATHER AND CHILD
Old Oraibi — c. 1895

It is easy to see that these people live in houses made of adobe mud, since they have the stuff dried on parts of their bodies. Perhaps this was a time when their houses were being repaired with wet mud, or it could be the result of some ceremonial activity at which time different colored earth powders are ritually rubbed on.

The hot desert life of these people is also evident by their lack of clothng, perhaps even by their hair styles. The old man would have had long hair down his back, which was usually kept rolled up behind the head in a bun except at ceremonial times.

Water was always a precious thing for the Hopi and baths a real luxury. For this reason the people treasured shells as symbols of water; this old man wears shell pieces around his neck and from his earlobes, among other small objects that were special to him.

CLIMBING THE PUEBLO LADDER
Hopi — Walpi Village, Arizona — 1906

"Hey, what's going on up here? Look, it's my cousin and my aunt — and there's my momma, too! She's watching me because it would hurt if I fall." That's what I imagine this little Hopi kid is saying to himself. Maybe he's heading up to play with his cousin: they might make little houses with wet clay.

When I was younger, we once visited relatives at a pueblo and I climbed ladders like this one. I remember that they seemed to go way up high and that we slept in a little room upstairs. The whole place was made with adobe mud and the people were still living like the ones in this picture. We watched some of their dances and ceremonial foot races that have been held since ancient times — since way before this photo was taken. We learned that there are still several of these old pueblos being lived in.

GROUP OF HOPI CHILDREN
First Mesa, Arizona
c. 1890

Wonder what persuaded this bunch of kids to line up and pose on the roof of their adobe pueblo house? The photographoer must not have worked fast enough, with his big tripod and box camera, since some of them moved during the slow exposure — or else they were too anxious to leave.

It's interesting to think that some of these kids could be the great-great-grandparents of someone now about my age. I guess back then they were much less shy about going around the way nature made them, especially the boys. This was true with most tribes, at least until missionaries came and said it was a sin to be seen the way you were born.

The girls in this picture are all wearing traditional Hopi dresses of homemade wool, on which one shoulder was left free. Imagine how it felt to have that rough wool next to the skin all through the hot desert days! I'm sure glad soft cloth and leather are used for most traditonal dresses nowadays.

OUT FOR A BURRO RIDE
Old Oraibi Village — Arizona
Hopi — c. 1895
Photo by George Wharton James

Looks like this Hopi grandpa has his hands full! You can imagine burros don't usually carry such heavy loads; most likely that old man uses it to haul water from distant springs, plus wood for the cooking fires. In the fall he would use it to bring home the corn and other things that grow in his desert garden. The photographer probably tempted him with a few coins to overload the poor animal just for this picture. The burro was probably glad when all this was over, so it could go lay down somewhere in the shade.

The old grandpa and a couple of the kids are dressed in traditional Hopi style, while the boy on the back wears store-bought clothes and has short-cropped hair, probably from attending a missionary school. In contrast, the one at the front must have really been enjoying this hot day! In the background, a little girl and her dad appear to be doing some neighborhood visiting, along with their spotted dog.

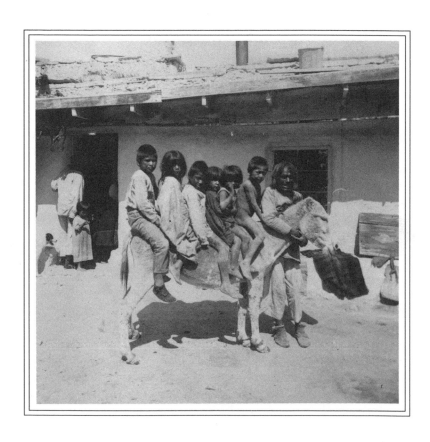

HOPI CHIEF AND GIRLS
Arizona — c. 1890
Photo by George Wharton James

We can only wonder what might have brought these five girls to pose with their old chief, whose name is recorded as being Lamonyaoma. Perhaps it was a ceremonial occasion, since Hopi women have always been important participants in their people's dances and sacred events, starting at childhood. All have their hair in the traditional Hopi style, rolled in two blossoms at the sides, and they are wearing homemade woolen dresses along with thin shawls and many strings of beads.

The Hopi people have lived for ages in several neighboring villages perched on top of steep mesas in the Arizona desert. Marauding enemies were always a threat, although they could usually be seen from a long ways off. Those who managed to reach the mesa tops were still faced with buildings that originally had no windows or ground level openings, each home being entered through the top by ladders like the one at the left, which would be hauled up in times of danger. The stone stairway on the right probably did not exist in those days.

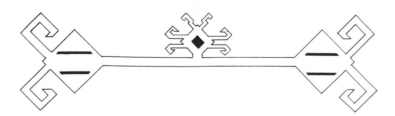

THE NATURE OF MOTHERHOOD
Hopi, Arizona
Photo by Edward S. Curtis

Wherever this mother goes, her child comes along, riding comfortably at her back, feeling wanted and a part of something. Spending a lot of time playing down on the ground, this high-up perch also gives the child a different view of life, a better idea of how things will be in adulthood.

So many children in today's world grow up without such intimate daily experiences, their parents gone to work or to do other things all day, or even worse, with their parents just plain gone. Perhaps if this classic photo by such a well-known lensman is seen often enough, it will continue to inspire the occasional mother to spend more time with her child during that early bonding period when she can still carry it around.

HOPI GIRL
Old Oraibi Village, Arizona — c. 1895

This could be thought of as a desolate scene if one didn't know how pueblo villages have evolved over time. Walls and homes built many centuries ago often stand beside others whose builders are alive today. In the hundred years since this picture was taken, some family may have reconstructed the fallen down parts seen here while the active house on the right could now be crumbling to pieces. Old Oraibi is among the most ancient villages still being used in North America.

For ages Hopi women and girls wore woolen dresses like this one, leaving one shoulder free and tying a colorful sash around the waist. This scene is almost timeless, since the girl's grandmother would have looked about the same in her time. However, if this girl had grandchildren, chances are they only wore dresses like this at ceremonial occasions, as many Hopi girls and women still do. Modern clothing is worn by most Hopis at other times, though some dedicated individuals prefer traditional wear.

At the same time, this picture demonstrates different aspects of pueblo construction. Some villages are built up basically with logs and adobe bricks, but here the custom is to use flat stones to give the adobe walls their strength. The wall on the right shows the finished work, wherein fresh layers of mud mixed with straw are applied every year. Of special note is the fact that no large trees grow on or near the Hopi mesas, so that every log seen on a building represents a great deal of effort, having been carried from distant forests by Hopi men, sometimes helped by burros.

HOPI MADONNA

"Silas' wife — 1901 — Nufwunci and her baby
at the Hopi village of Mishongnovi, Arizona"

This mother appears thoughtful as she rests in the doorway of her adobe home and suckles her child. In a few minutes she'll have to go back inside to her flour grinding and bread making which she does kneeling, as can be seen from the work stains on the upper parts of her woolen dress. The child will rejoin playmates frolicking carefree in the hot desert sun.

Hopi women are noted for their fine basketry, pottery and other work, some of which Nufwunci has displayed here. Back then these things were part of everyday pueblo life, but nowadays they are valuable works of art. A scene like this could still be photographed. Hopi people are among the most dedicated Indians practicing their own traditional ways. They regard their ancient mesa-top villages as sacred places within which they still hold frequent ceremonials.

NAVAJO BOY
Arizona — c. 1890

This traditional looking, long-haired boy reminds us of the famous Navajo Hosteen Klah, who lived at about the same time. He began learning the complex rituals of his people before he was ten years old, making him a genius and role model for future generations of Navajos.

Hosteen Klah's parents kept him home from government schools where other Navajo kids were sent, so that he could help care for an elderly uncle who taught him his ways. Together they travelled around their desert homeland, as the old man was called by various families to lead rituals, which the boy thus learned. Along trails they gathered medicinal roots and plants, which was also part of his education.

Later, Hosteen Klah was sent to help an old aunt and uncle from among the related Apaches, with whom he learned another important ritual. When he returned home from there, he was asked to heal an injured younger boy who had been struck by lightning. Using the five-day Hail Chant, Hosteen performed the healing successfully and thereby gained a reputation that he kept for the rest of his life. Among other accomplishments, he wove elaborate rugs based on some ritual details, which can still be seen in several museums. Before he died, he also helped write a book about his life.

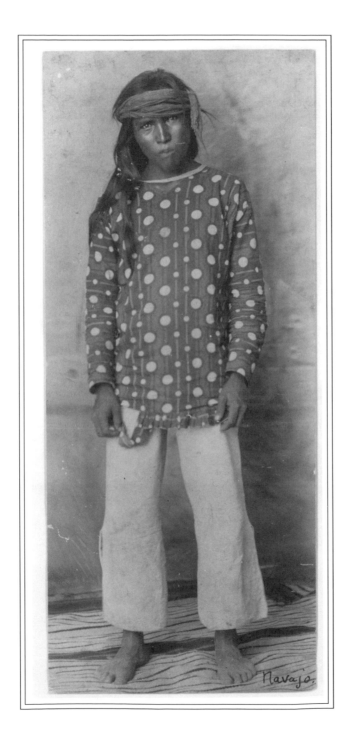

Navajo.

NAVAJO BABY TRAVEL
Gallup, New Mexico — c. 1900
Photo by Pennington

"My goodness, what was that fire shooting up from the end of your hand?" this kid seems to be asking the studio photographer, while his mom doesn't look particularly thrilled by the experience. Maybe it's his grandma, wanting him to have a picture so someday he could see how she looked when he was a baby. Wonder what remote desert trails they normally travelled; this might have been the kid's first visit to the white man's world.

The woman wears one of the many beautiful designs still being produced on blankets and shawls by the Pendelton Woolen Mills in Oregon, some of which are now very valuable and scarce.

"NAVAJO MOTHER AND BABE IN CRADLE"
Arizona — c. 1925
Photo by Ruth Moran

It seems like this mom and her kid are doing something special becuse of the fancy clothes and silver jewelry, but I've heard that many Navajo women dressed like this even when they were alone, tending their herds of sheep way out on the desert. Anyhow, they sure are a proud and good looking pair.

This baby was wrapped in a good blanket and then strapped to its willow board. There was a soft-tanned hide thrown back over the canopy; the mother would lower it over the baby while it was sleeping. This also helped keep flies and bugs from being bothersome.

Silverwork is a craft for which the Navajo are widely noted; among their specialties are conch belts and squash-blossom necklaces, both of which this mother wears. Like most women, she probably also wove rugs, for which the tribe is even more famous. These are crafts that continue to provide cultural pride along with income for many families.

NAVAJO FAMILY
Arizona desert — c. 1925

These two kids must have enjoyed trips to the trading post with their parents, since Navajo family homes are scattered far and wide across the hills and deserts. Candy treats were no doubt available for those who behaved — maybe even a toy now and then — while dad looked for useful things like tools, rope or bullets and mother checked out the kitchen section and materials for clothing. Note that they're all wearing store-bought shoes here, though back home around their hogan and herds of sheep they probably used traditional hard-soled, high-topped moccasins.

Long ago, the Navajo migrated down to their hot Southwest desert country from way up North, learning a new and different lifestyle. Joined along the way by small groups of other native people, some of whom brought their own skills and customs, they are now North America's largest Indian tribe, with a reservation that lies in parts of four states: Arizona, New Mexico, Colorado and Utah. With well over 100,000 members, they speak of themselves as the Navajo Nation. In Canada their relatives are the Sarcee and the numerous Dene of the Northwest Territories.

"READY TO ENJOY VACATION"
Mohave, Arizona — c. 1890
Photo by George Wharton James

Girls of the desert, apparently at school, since the photographer mentioned their vacation. They would be going back ot their reservation homes and helping in the gardens, as their people always relied heavily on crops such as corn, pumpkins, melons, beans and wheat. Desert hunting provided only limited amounts of meat, but mesquite beans and wild nuts were regularly gathered.

Mohave girls and women share an interesting tradition, in that they all carry one of about twenty names that have been handed down among them over the ages. Since the people sometimes numbered three or four thousand, this must have provided occasional confusion and memorable meetings. Of couse, the girls in this picture would have all had English names of their own, so the teachers and government poeple could keep track of them. But in their own language at home, several would no doubt have been called the same name from among those twenty choices.

These girls wear several styles of native cloth dresses, though back in the times of their grandmothers they would have used very little clothing. Mohaves were a proud people which can be seen by the neat and traditonal appearance of these girls, whose forefathers were widely respected as brave warriors defending their families and Colorado River lands from constant marauders.

101

CHEMEHUEVI MOTHER AND CHILD
Colorado River — c. 1895
C. C. Pierce and Co. Photographers, Los Angeles

This pretty young mother appears to be settled on one of the reservation rancherias where most of her tribe was by then living, although some families kept their "wild" roaming lifestyle into the early 1900's. Chemehuevi territory was in the deserts and dry hills along the Colorado River, so this lady knew very hot days and sometimes strong sandstorms.

The cradleboard is of a common southwestern style similar to that of other tribes. White bird plumes adorn the woven shade that protects the baby's head.

Perhaps they were of help in keeping insects away as they fluttered in the breezes, but they may also have had some particular spiritual meaning as most bird and animal things do for Native American people. Chemehuevi, incidentally are of Shoshonean stock and related to the more numerous Paiute.

103

PAIUTE ELDER WITH GRANDSON
Nevada Desert — c. 1878
Photo by Hiller — Smithsonian Institute

From what I've learned about the Paiute people, this boy is receiving his initiation as a young hunter from his father or grandfather (not necessarily a blood relative — any special elder might be called by these terms). See how new and white his buckskin suit is, as compared to the old man's well-worn shirt and leggings, darkened by lots of campfire smoke and outdoor living. Paiute men did all the sewing, even on women's dresses.

Upon return home after his first successful hunt, the boy will be bathed by his mother and his body ceremonially painted red. He will be first to taste the meat, but will only spit the bite into the fire for hope of continued success, while his parents do the actual eating.

Note that the boy has a wolf or coyote tail attached to the bow and quiver at his back — a good luck symbol from animals known to be skillful hunters. What might he be saying at a moment like this?

"You should have stayed at the camp, instead of disturbing us out here with your Magic Box and your noisy shoes. Grandfather is teaching me ways of silence! However, yesterday we had no hunting success, so he says your Magic Box might change our luck for the better. Go ahead then and take your picture, so we can get back to what we were doing — singing our special songs and performing the hunting ceremony. Soon the Sun will be setting; that's when the rabbits and quail will come out."

PAIUTE BABY IN CRADLEBOARD
Bishop, California — c. 1915
Photo by Forbes Studio

This baby looks kind of big to still be in a cradleboard, but I guess that I was about two before I stayed out of mine. See the shoes; that baby can probably walk, like I did around that age.

In traditional Indian camps there were no cribs or beds; instead, cradleboards were used to hold babies safely, especially while they were sleeping or when the family was on the move. I don't have any memories of being inside my own, but my mom and dad tell me that I was very happy in there.

Before a baby is tied to its cradleboard, it is first snugly wrapped up in a blanket. Leather thongs are usually used to tie it on, but in this case they have used a sash instead. In the past they often carried the baby around just in the wrapping, made out of soft buckskin. We call this a moss bag, because they used to put cleaned moss into it for a diaper padding. My mom's aunt Mary One Spot made a beaded one of these which I was put in around home instead of my cradleboard.

The Paiutes and other southwestern tribes used willow sticks to make the frames of their cradleboards, like this one. It looks like lots of work and a nice result. Up north here by us, most of the tribes used solid boards to make theirs.

"Harry Brown — 1st Prise
for Health for Babies Under One Year"
"Piute Indian Baby Show — Bishop, California, 1916"
Photo by Forbes Studio, Bishop

"Yippee, I won!" says this happy-looking little Paiute kid. "They say I'm the healthiest of the bunch, here at the country fair." Can you imagine going to a public event nowadays where they have competition for the healthiest babies of a certain race? Back then it probably seemed like a good idea to the organizers for getting local native people involved in the surrounding community.

One of the biggest challenges to the survival of Indian people in the early reservation years was the high rate of infant mortality. This was due to a number of reasons, including illnesses brought by the oncoming settlers and the change of lifestyle from wandering in Nature to being cooped up on reservations. For that reason, perhaps awarding prizes for especially healthy babies was done to encourgage mothers to maintain healthy practices as part of their new, imposed lifestyles.

PAIUTE BOY AND GIRL
c. 1876

Growing up as "Desert Children," young Paiutes had a very tough life. Their people roamed parts of Arizona, Nevada, Utah and Oregon often so remote that many Paiute bands remained unknown and unseen by non-Indians until well into the 1800's, which is late for any tribe.

Much of Paiute country had so little to offer in food, water and plants that early white settlers passed it by; even the Indians often lived with hunger and thirst. Staying alive took so much effort that the people had lttle time to develop a complex culture; clothing remained simple, as did ceremonies and legends. When first seen by outsiders, these native people seemed not much different from those found in ancient caves and desert burials, who might have also been Paiute ancestors from thousands of years before.

Mythical red-haired cannibals were the feared neighbors and enemies of the ancient Paiute; legends of battles and other encounters with them survive, including tales of how they were finally destroyed by the northern branch of Paiutes. They were known as Pine Nut Eaters because a favorite food of the people is the Pinyon nut. It was eaten raw in great quantities, or else cooked into a meal or ground up and made into sort of a bread.

The red-haired cannibals used to "waylay the Indians and devour them," old people said, while gathering pine nuts, or even while sleeping at home. They could jump into the air and catch arrows that were shot at them. But eventually the people joined in a strong force, surrounded their savage enemies on the shore of a lake, and began to kill them off. Those who escaped managed to hide in a protected cave. The people then blocked its entrace with logs and set up a guard. When patience wore out, they set fire to the blockade and thus destroyed the inhabitants. From this they took the name Say-do-carah, Conquerors.

Young Paiute People Gather to Play the Handgame
Utah desert country — c. 1878

At every pow-wow we've been to, the peculiar songs of the handgame were heard day and night from the outskirts of the camp. The main traditional form of Indian gambling, it is still very popular throughout North America. One of its main attractions is the money that is exchanged through betting, sometimes very big sums. But there is als a lot of spirit and drama among the players, plus the more modern addition of formal intertribal championships.

Here's how the game looked while played among the desert-dwelling Paiutes over one hundred years ago. Having stood and watched such players as these, here's what we imagine one of these kids to say:

"My older brother says these guys are crazy, throwing their belongings away just to play a game. They gamble coins, guns, knives, even their horses, trying to outguess each other about a hidden marked bone. See the fellow pointing, with one arm out and the other over his heart? He's trying to feel for power, so that his finger will be led to point where the bone is. The guy with his arms inside his blanket, sitting opposite, has the marked bone in one of his hands.

"They sing while they're doing this, a kind of hypnotizing chant without any real words. They move around and try to distract each other. Watching them is fun, but my brother would never allow me to take part. He is a proud hard worker who thinks everyone else should be too. You can recognize him in this crowd by his fancy beaded shirt and neatly combed hair, which is how he thinks a grown Paiute man should properly dress. He says gamblers dress shabby, like us younger boys, wasting their time instead of helping their families prosper. When I grow up I will be a proud warrior like my brother, not throwing away my goods like these foolish men.

"But meanwhile, their game is just about over and their singing is kind of drawing my attention, so if you don't mind..."

"KLICKITAT INDIANS ON COLUMBIA RIVER"
"Washington State — between 1907 & 1910"

Fish-loving people were the Klickitats, which is probably why they were camped here along the Columbia River. Most likely this grandma was roasting some slabs of salmon over the open fire which is barely visible next to the coffee pot. At least four kids are in the picture behind her; the pleasant look on her face may be one reason why; another is that she was probably generous with her smoked salmon. She may have kept berries or sweets in that pretty basket by her side, which she may also have made, since Klickitats are noted basket weavers.

Perhaps the shy girl beside her was her favorite, they must have sat together sometimes and told stories. The old lady would recall steamboats bringing strangers up and down the Columbia, while the girl might tell of far-away places learned about in school. Although they are here in the same camp, imagine how different their experiences were in everyday life.

Klickitat territory in Washington State includes the famous volcano, Mount St. Helens, which they called "Loo-wit." According to tribal myths, Loo-wit was a faithful old woman who guarded the so called Bridge of the Gods and was rewarded by the Great Spirit with an eternally youthful form. Because of a horrible battle back in ancient times, Loo-wit withdrew from the main mountain range and settled by herself far to the west, where Klickitat Indians always thought of her as the youngest and most beautiful looking, yet the oldest in age of all snow mountains.

TW-WAH-Y
Yakima tribe, Washington State
Photo by L. V. McWhorter — c. 1910

This baby's cradleboard is certainly a work of art, though close inspection reveals some odd characteristics that seem intended more for the photographer's appreciation than actual use. For instance, the main wrapper of velvet, with its beautiful floral beadwork, is actually a man's fancy vest! Sleeve openings can be seen at the top sides, while the front has quite an overlap but is missing the lacing usually found on cradles to hold the child in. A shawl wrapped around the lower portion helps hide the fact that this interesting looking contraption has no enclosed bottom.

Chances are the vest was neatly draped over an actual cradle covering that was considered too plain for the photo, although the oval "roll-bar" for protecting the baby's head is decorated with two kinds of beads, plus dangling metal tokens obtained from a trading post in Toppenish, Washington (readable with a magnifying glass!) on the Yakima reservation. Barely visible behind this rounded stick is the stylistically-carved top of the wooden cradle-board itself, shaped somewhat like the hilt of a large dagger. Part of it is covered by a double-strand of white wampum beads, again added for temporary decoration. The same is true for the necklace and shell around the baby's neck, probably part of the mother's jewelry collection, along with the baby's "headband" of dentalium shells and brass beads, actually a choker whose large round shell would hang down from the front of an adult's neck. The pleasant look on this dark-eyed youngster's face indicates that it wasn't much disturbed by all the added nonsense.

TW-WAH-Y   6 MO OLD
COPYRIGHT BY L.V. MC. WHORTER

"CARDING WOOL"
Yakima Indians — Photographed August, 1918
by L. V. McWhorter

It's around the end of the first world war; virtually all the tribes had some young men who fought in it; among them was no doubt a relative of this old woman, perhaps even a son or grandson. As in the warpath days of old, she would have thought about that individual every day and prayed for his successful return.

Yet, the actual images of that war would have been practically beyond her imagination. Life for her revolved around Yakima customs, centered upon salmon taken from the Columbia River, along whose banks the people built longhouses and camped in tipis, which they still do regularly. As can be seen from the well-built house in this photo, these people accepted the new ways of arriving settlers without losing the best parts of their own traditions. Nowadays they have among the finest dance costumes and sponsor frequent pow-wows. In contrast to the poverty of some tribes, they have been very successful at such business operations as fruit growing and ranching. Yet they continue to draw spiritual strength from ceremonies and faiths based on nature and inherited from their ancestors.

This girl looks like she might be home from boarding school to visit her grandma. By her store-bought clothing you might think she has given up her tribal customs. No doubt, that's what her school teachers would have wanted.

But the Yakima have been among those tribes across North America with members who attended schools but returned later to some of their traditional ways, including dress. Therefore, it may well be that this girl looked about the same as her old grandma, when she reached that age.

117

PLATEAU GROUP
WEEKDAY DRESS
c. 1910

This is one of those common old photos with no writng or information whatsoever. By the looks of this print and a couple of others that go with it, these kids belong to one of the Plateau tribes in Idaho or Washington and were photographed around the turn of the century.

We might imagine they are standing in front of a trading post, where some passing photographer posed them together. We can tell that this was still in the early reservation period (1880's to 1920's) because most of these boys have long hair and several are wearing leggings, moccasins and blankets. At that time they would have played and even gone to school this way.

PLATEAU GROUP
SUNDAY DRESS
c. 1910

Taken at what appears to be the same time and area as the previous photo, this scene shows some young native people dressed in the latest store-bought fashion, much different from their everyday tradtional dress at home.

Possibly this is a missionary building and they're on their way to church. In those days it would have been common for at least some of them to come home from church and then participate in a traditonal ceremony as well. In fact, some native poeple still do that today.

PLATEAU INDIAN BOY
Washington State — c. 1900

Dear Pen Pal:

Thank you for send letter to me. English not so good, but will try best I can. Don't know place you live, but heard the name. Must be big city, lotsa people. Out here, not so much people, maybe few hundreds.

You ask my picture, so teacher in school took for me. Took for other fellows with pen pals too. My folks told me, wear best blanket, you see it; got lotsa colors.

You ask what I do after school. Just help folks farm, raise up horses, got couple cows, lots potatoes and carrots. Best time is when I go with friends to dancing, what we call pow-wow. Get dressed up fancy, wear beaded costume like my dad's, jingling bells on legs, feathers in hair. But know what I like best in pow-wow? Lotsa girls. You want me tell you about pow-wow girls? You tell me about city girls first, then I tell you. O.K.?

Your friend Barnaby

SPOKANE BOYS
Washington State — c. 1920

These two little fellows don't look too thrilled about having their picture taken, although they are dressed very nicely for the purpose, wearing typical Plateau style clothing. Traditional Spokane country was in the vicinity of today's city by the same name, surrounded by tribes with similar clothing styles and cultural customs. They were a tipi-dwelling, horse-riding people who hunted and fished in the mountains and valleys, with occasional trips to the Plains for buffalo. The name Spokane is said to mean "Children of the Sun."

Notice the different bits of animal fur worn by these boys; these were considered symbols of good luck by their people. A piece of coyote tail hangs from the bandolier across the chest of the taller boy, suggesting that he should acquire the clever cunning of that animal. Spokane mythology tells how animals were here on earth long before people, with Coyote being considered the most important of them. Even though kids knew Coyote best as the legendary trickster, elders say he also did more than any other animal to make the world better.

CULTURAL MIX
Washington State — c. 1920

It may be that these two little girls still wore native dresses around their home and considered it a special treat to put on new style clothing for this photograph. Even so, there are several traditional items such as the bead necklace, bracelet, moccasins and of course the fancy toy cradleboard. It has a fully beaded top of typical Plateau style and even a decorated buckskin flap covering the body of the cradle.

Even with their modern appearance, these kids would have been well acquainted with tales of Coyote, who annoyed people and animals alike in an endless series of escapades told by the fireside. Their parents probably scared them into behaving with statements like, "Coyote will come and get you if you don't straighten up."

What You Laughing About?
Spokane Tribe, Washington — c. 1920

That baby seems less thrilled about the picture-taking than the older fellow, who can barely hold still long enough. This is part of a series of picture taken of Spokane kids at the same time, although the photographer failed to record names and information. Perhaps some of these kids are still living and will recognize themselves, although they would now be quite old.

From museum research we learn that Spokane cradleboards like this one are of the same style as those used by other Plateau tribes and even the neighboring Blackfeet. They are typically about three feet tall, 15 inches wide at the top, with a main board less than an inch thick and tapered towards the bottom. A soft deerskin hide is stretched tightly across the whole back and down the upper third of the front, where it is usually decorated with fine beadwork. The lower two thirds of the front formed two flaps that covered the occupant and were laced together snugly by leather strings criss-crossed through a series of loops.

The back part of this cradle is decorated with a row of leather fringe hanging down from near the top to a point where a wide strap is attached to the board in such a manner that the mother can wear it over her back, hang it from her saddle when riding, or else from a tree branch while working nearby.

To the upper part of the two laced-up flaps there is a hood of leather or cloth to shelter the baby's head. To this hood are attached little medicine bags, shells, strings of beads and other things to entertain the child and give it spritual protection. Of course, the child was first wrapped up in soft material before being laced into this practical structure.

BIG SMALL, LITTLE SMALL
Spokane Tribe, Washington — c. 1920

Cradleboards like these are so practical that they are still used today. It is assumed that they are of an ancient style, probably decorated with colored porcupine quills before the coming of beads, but otherwise made about the same. The arrival of settlers brought lumber, eliminating the tedious chore of carving the main board by hand from a tree.

Flower designs were most common on beaded cradleboards, with many hours spent filling in the fine designs. Part of a bead-decorated belt is seen at the back, where it served as a carrying strap, worn across the mother's shoulders and chest. The strings of beads attached below the baby's face were probably a loop necklace of the style worn by the happy boy standing there. He has on a store-bought vest, a fringed breechcloth made from a shawl, plus typical Plateau style leggings and moccasins.

"HUNTER"
Coeur d'Alene Indian Tribe, Idaho — c. 1910

Perhaps this picture should have been titled "Hunters," since the little boy behind his dad is holding a pistol as though he's wishing he'd been able to use it on the deer that will provide some weeks of food for his family. Actually, the photographer probably posed this scene after the lone hunter returned, since boys this small would have been more of a burden than help. The same goes for the puppy behind the boy, although the dog on the ground is attached to a good rawhide leash which indicates that it was probably trained for tracking quarry such as deer and elk in the Plateau country of this man's tribe.

Although the clothing, rifle and riding gear has modern influence, back when this man was his son's age he would have still worn buckskins and been proficient with bow and arrow. He may even have ridden like this with his own father during one of their tribe's occasional long journeys out to the great Plains where they hunted buffalo for meat and especially for the warm hides.

HUNTER - Coe..rd'Alene Indian Tribe A

"FRONTIER DAYS WARRIORS"
Walla Walla, Washington — c. 1920

Although the photographer has romantically designated these dancers as "warriors," most of them are much too young to have actually been on the warpath, since those days ended some forty years earlier for these people. However, a number of dancers are carrying spears which might symbolize past participation in war-like activities. Some of them are old enough to have participated themselves, while others may be dancing in honor of their fathers or grandfathers, which was sometimes a common practice.

Long hair was still the popular style for grown-up men in this region, but the two boys on the right show their school influence with short hair, yet their dance outfits are just as traditional as the rest.

Although nowadays girls and women dance right along with the men at pow-wows the traditional custom was for them to form a circle of their own and dance proudly together, as can be seen here in the background. Sometimes it has been said that Indian dances at events like this Walla Walla Frontier Days were performed only for the sake of non-native spectators, but Indians usually like to dance at any time and this public event was probably just considered another good opportunity to do so.

16. Frontier Days Warriors Walla Walla Wn. "Bawgus"

PHOTO DAY AT THE TRADING POST
Plateau Father and Son
Idaho — c. 1915

We might imagine that this man knew there was going to be a photographer at the trading post, since his boy is dressed in ornate fashion. The boy's decorated shirt has bunches of weasel skins which carry ceremonial meaning beyond their decorative value. Weasels are swift and silent hunters; any father would want his boy to have those attributes.

The father is holding up his son's hand to show that weasel tails are attached there and to his necklace, which indicates an exceptionally strong wish for this boy to grow closer to weasels. The spiritual power he may have gained from this would have served him later in adulthood to become a medicine man, sharing healings and advice. It was usually men who already had such powers that most encouraged their children to also seek them.

PLATEAU INDIAN GIRL
c. 1915

The Plateau people dressed and looked a lot like tribes of the Plains, where they sometimes went to hunt buffalo, but their home country was in the hills and valleys of the Northwest, between the Rocky Mountains and the Pacific Coast. Here, life was usually more peaceful and less disturbed. Among Plateau tribes were the Nez Perce, Spokane, Flathead, Kootenay, Umatilla, Cayuse and others.

Clothing features especially popular with Plateau people are large round conch shells like this girl has on her necklace. Like the women and girls of most tribes, she also has her shawl, in this case a fringed woolen one worn around the waist. Until just recently some old Plateau women still dressed like this all the time, but now the traditional styles are saved mainly for special occasions such as pow-wows and other tribal ceremonials.

NEZ PERCE GIRL AND HER AUNT
"CHILD OF BLIND INDIAN WOMAN"
Lapwai, Idaho — c. 1910

These people lived in forests and valleys of the Northwest where elk were considered very noble animals. This girl has a row of canine elk teeth sewn to her special woolen dress. Some hunter cared for her a lot — perhaps her father or uncle — since each elk has only two of these teeth.

The aunt must have decided that a photo would be good for the girl to have as a keepsake, so she got her dressed in finest traditional wear, although her own clothing is rather plain. It must have been a memorable experience for an Indian kid to be brought into a studio, where strangers worked with odd equipment and sudden flashes, surrounded by huge, make-believe, hand-painted scenes.

"NEZ PERCE CHILDREN —
NANCY AND KATE EDWARDS"
Oregon — c. 1900

Many tribes liked trading with the Nez Perce for their finely woven cornhusk bags, such as the two decorated ones held by these girls. They were used to store many things, including dried roots, berries and other foods, plus sewing gear and ceremonial articles. Children were taught at a young age how to do this unique art, which some members of the tribe continue to produce today.

People of the Plateau tribes such as the Nez Perce had exceptionally thick hair, perhaps helped by their custom of rubbing fish oil and other natural substances into it. Another custom was to wear a lot of shells, such as the round ones these girls have on their earrings and necklaces. Traditionlly, these people also wore thin shells through their noses, which is how they received their tribal name which means in French, Pierced Nose.

This picture was taken in a studio about 25 years after the famous battles between U.S. army troops and groups of Nez Perce led by the highly-regarded Chief Joseph, who was trying to lead his people up to Canada after the U.S. government swindled them out of promised hereditary lands due to pressures from incoming settlers. The Nez Perce are also credited as a main source for the famous Appaloosa horses.

NEZ PERCE BOY
Pendelton, Oregon — c. 1915

One reason the Nez Perce were strong people is that boys not too much older than this one were sent out alone into the wilderness for days or even weeks at a time, carrying no food and sleeping on the ground under trees at night. In this way they sought spiritual instructions through dreams and visions that helped guide their lives.

Many tribes of Plateau Indians live around the city of Pendelton, where they have gathered every Fall for decades to celebrate at a famous rodeo, pow-wow and fair called Pendelton Roundup. Perhaps this boy had his picture taken during that time, when many people dress up in their finest costumes.

U13 OREGON INDIAN BOY.

GROUP OF FLATHEAD CHILDREN
Western Montana — c. 1895

Looks like these kids couldn't decide between themselves whether they wanted to pose for this picture or not.
The little guy in the middle definitely decided *not*, based on
his teary looking face. Notice that he and the two guys on his
left all have weasel skins hanging from their shoulders. At
this time the Flathead people still spent a lot of time out in
Nature, hunting and gathering wild foods, even though they
had permanent homes on their reservation. Kids learned
about Nature by living in it — as in the "old days" — and
parents encouraged them to seek spirtual companionship
with different birds and animals, whose feathers and skins
were sometimes attached to hair or clothing.

Long hair for boys and girls was still the common
Flathead style then, although this girl has her hair cropped
unusually short, which suggests that she may have been
treated for vermin. By their plain, well-worn moccasins, we
can also tell that they are dressed in everyday clothing. For
girls this meant long cloth dresses (buckskin was saved for
special occasions once cloth became common). Boys wore
breechcloths on belts, with long shirts that covered them,
plus cloth leggings with side flaps and decorated panels
around the ankles. Kids' clothing was similar to that of
Flathead adults, with styles that were also common among
such neighboring tribes as the Blackfeet and most of the
Plateau people.

Girls, if you find the little fellow on the left kind of cute,
with his striped shirt, three little braids and funky hat, then
you're probably wishing you'd been there a hundred years
ago to find out why he's wearing that necklace with an
abalone shell heart.

FLATHEAD FATHER AND SONS
Helena, Montana Territory — c. 1885
Photo by Moriarty — Sunbeam Studio
Galen Block — Main Street foot of Broadway

Our old Flathead friend Louie Ninepipe is the one who told us this was a father and his two sons, although he couldn't remember their names. He was born around the time this picture was taken, when the Flatheads still followed their traditional way of life in the valleys and mountains of Western Montana, especially around the Bitterroot River and its ranges. He had pictures like this taken with his own dad and brothers, during one of their rare trips into the "white man's towns." He figured the younger boy probably had candy in that paper sack he's holding — that's what he used to look forward to most about going to town.

That these people still lived mostly outdoors is one reason they are wearing bullets belts; also, sometimes they were given a hard time in town by rough cowboys or men coming from saloons. Note that the father is carrying a pistol on his belt up front, though Flatheads were known as peaceful people, usually willing to be friends.

Ladies' shawls were popular with them for breechcloths because they were soft and warm, besides having colorful plaid designs and fringes that hung down. Most men wore their hair in braids, while the younger one often cut bangs which they sometimes trained to stand upright, just to look stylish, like this boy has done. We wonder if he gave a picture like this to one of his girlfriends?

ANDREW WOODCOCK AND CHILD
Pend Oreille Tribe, Idaho — c. 1895

This man was known among his own people by the name Little Blackfoot, although they were normally enemies of that tribe, especially when the two met each other while buffalo hunting on the open prairie. The Pend Oreille lived most of the time peacefully and by themselves in the forests and mountains west of the Rockies, where a lake and a city has been named after them.

Little Blackfoot was a noted healer or medicine man. One badge of his office is the bunch of white weasel skins attached to his right shoulder, along with a piece of coyote tail and some little round leather pouches containing his sacred herbs. When this picture was taken it was still common for men like him to go around wearing beaded loop necklaces and metal arm bands, along with blankets in place of coats. The ends of his long hair are wrapped with otter fur, which was a popular style.

Looks like this baby will grow quite a bit before it gets too big for its cradleboard, which was possibly handed down from an older sibling. Think of all the work that went into making it — first in tanning the soft hide and sewing it to shape, then covering its large headboard with pretty designs and background colors of countless tiny beads. We could say this baby's portable home is truly a work of art.

TEACHING THE YOUNG TO RECORD
BLACKFOOT HISTORY
Glacier National Park — 1915
Photo by Hileman

Education was part of everyday life for the children of native tribes, who were always around their parents, grandparents and elders. They learned by watching and doing; instead of earning grades, they acquired skills which were necessary to continue in their traditional way.

Since native people had no written language, drawings were used to record important events. This man is touching up a picture of an elk, perhaps an exceptionally large one that he once shot. Other figures illustrate memories from his warpath days, along with creatures from mystical dreams that gave him guidance in life.

Watching quietly the boy would have learned the meanings of such drawings, at the same time being inspired to seek similar experiences in his own grown-up life. Unfortunately for him, the Blackfeet — like other Indians — were then seeing the end of the life illustrated by these drawings, their days replaced by less picturesque experiences.

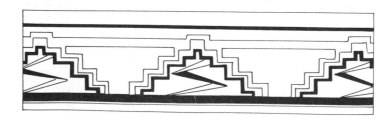

151

Camp of the Siksika
A division of the Blackfoot Confederacy
Bow River, Alberta — c. 1880

These boys were probably members of a traditional society whose meetings were held in the tipi behind them. Societies were handed down from one age group to the next, their members enjoying respect for serving as tribal police and defese forces. Blackfoot boys this young might have belonged to the Mosquitoes, Bees or Prairie Chickens, each of which had its own inherited songs, dances and other customs.

Most of the traditional societies died out in the years following reservation life, but some still meet, including one called the Brave Dogs, to which our family belongs. The meetings are usually held at night in the leader's tipi, set up in a distict spot within the camp circle. Fellowship is shared around a blazing fire in the form of lively discussion, plus the practice of society songs and dances. Nowadays at least, mothers and sisters often particpate as members, though in the past women's roles were more limited.

The big pile of firewood in front of this tipi indicates that the boys may be getting ready for their next meeting. The man standing to the left was probably their main advisor, a former member wise to the society's ways. He is puffing on a little pipe and holding a forked wooden tong that will be used during the gathering for bringing coals from the fire to an earth altar, where he will sprinkle dried sweetgrass for incense and make prayers.

The dots on this tipi represent stars in the night sky and were drawn according to some respected person's dreams and visions. The rights to put this design on a tipi are considered sacred and may be passed on to other people only through ceremonies that we still practice.

THREE PIKUNNI GIRLS
Glacier National Park — 1915

Although the buffalo days were over by the time of this picture, some families of the Pikunni brach of Blackfeet still practiced their tribal traditions during Summer encampments in Glacier National Park, at the edge of their reservation. They were encouraged to put up their tipis, perform dances and wear native clothing for the benefit of visitors and tourists.

These girls are recognizable as Blackfeet by the styles and decorations of their dresses. However, they are made of cloth obtained from stores, whereas their grandmothers wore mainly buckskin clothing of an older type. Theirs could have been hand-tanned and usually decorated with colored porcupine quills, while the ones seen here illustrate an assortment of beads and shells obtained by trade.

STAR AND HER GRANDMAS
Blood Indian Reserve, Alberta — 1982
Photo by Adolf Hungry Wolf

This is one of my favorite pictures from when I was a little girl, because it shows my Grandma Ruth Little Bear and my great-Grandma Hilda Strangling Wolf, who died a few years ago when she was almost 100. I feel very fortunate to remember her; she used to sing oldtime lullabye songs for me.

My Grandma Ruth's other name is Pretty Crow Woman, which was given to her in the Blackfoot language as a little girl. Great-grandma Hilda was named Pretty Woman; she grew up in the household of a warrior and medicine man named Heavy Head. Her real dad was a German trader who married my great-great-Grandma back in the buffalo days. They had several kids before they split up; then my great-great-Grandma remarried to Heavy Head, who took these children just like his own. He was a kind man who died at old age when my own mom was born.

My Grandpa Ed Little Bear gave me the Indian name of his Grandma, Sacred Pipe Woman, which is what I'm called when someone is speaking Blackfoot. This picture was taken at the back of our family's tent in a Blackfoot pow-wow camp.

INDEX

These fine Native American books are available from:
THE BOOK PUBLISHING COMPANY
PO Box 99
Summertown, TN 38483

Basic Call to Consciousness $7.95
§ Blackfoot Craftworker's Book $11.95
§ Children of the Circle $9.95
Dream Feather $9.95
§ A Good Medicine Collection:
    Life in Harmony with Nature $9.95
    How Can One Sell the Air? $4.95
§ Indian Tribes of the Northern Rockies $9.95
§ Legends Told By The Old People $5.95
A Natural Education $5.95
The People: Native American Thoughts and Feelings $5.95
The Powwow Calendar (Annual) $5.95
Song of the Seven Herbs $10.95
Spirit of the White Bison $5.95
§ Teachings of Nature $8.95
§ Traditional Dress $5.95

Please include $1.50 per book additional for shipping.

If you are interested in other fine books on Native Americans,
ecology, alternative health, gardening, vegetarian cookbooks, and
children's books, please call for a catalog:

1-800-695-2241

§ Good Medicine Books also available from:

GOOD MEDICINE BOOKS
Box 844
Skookumchuck, BC V0B 2E0 Canada

(Write for Canadian price and shipping information)